CW00420876

Simple Reality

by

Arsenio Di Donato

Copyright © 2019 Andy Karsai & Sandor Paal
Published by Donato Goods™
2nd English edition
All rights reserved!

Edited by Arsenio Di Donato

Cover art by Imagine

Table of Content

To My People

I have lived my life primarily alone, yet never lonely. At all different points of my life, intricate parts or easy ones, there always have been people near me, not necessarily physically near, but with kindness, goodness and care. They all significantly affected the good decisions I have made on my path.

It doesn't matter how much darkness surrounds you at times; from people or situations, there always have been, are and will be ones that will stand by you.

Those are the ones I will never forget.

No regrets!

To My Cats

Nothing but love.

About This Edition

I wrote this tale over two decades ago, on a weekend in 1996. I was young and had just passed twenty-three. Since then, I have made minor changes to that version, but the context, language, and mainly the phrases about IT and the internet have remained original, so those might sound weird today.

At the time of writing, the internet still had baby shoes on; Google, YouTube and Facebook were not even on the horizon; searching and finding any information worked substantially differently. Nevertheless, this trip back in time in the technical jargon should only make this story more interesting.

Thus, I wish you a pleasant couple of hours with this book while you embark on your journey with Andem.

"The parts of the universe all are connected with each other in such a way that I think it to be impossible to understand any one without the whole."

-- Blaise Pascal.

As Preface

I want to dedicate this book to the people searching for truth, fantasising about how this complicated and sometimes intimidating world works, and those who only accumulate and store information in their minds.

What you will read on the following pages might be a made-up story, but it can also happen in real life. I don't insist on either of those opinions; consider whatever you find more plausible. Towards the end, you shall figure out that the two are not that far apart. Regardless of which viewpoint we are observing this tale, it makes excellent food for thought.

I have spent a lot of time in the past years to figure out the world, to see the truth, which is not shown on the TV, in the newspaper, nor told by politicians or the people who rely on those mediums.

Centuries have passed with us only living for the show, behind a facade, the sheep mentality ruling over our minds, leading us into wars and catastrophes. I didn't want to accept that there was no way out, that everything shall happen the way it does, and that we could not do anything against it.

What is life? Why do we live? What is important; I mean actually important to us? Who could give us the answers to those questions without any manipulative or self-benefiting motives?

Since birth, I have constantly been told that life is not a game, I should work hard for my food and that life would always throw obstacles in my way that I could not deflect but would rather have to confront. Is it truly so? Then where would luck fit into the picture, that benevolent accident which helps people deal with their immediate problem?

What is luck, and why does it exist? What attracts accidental happenings? Why does one find a particular person instead of someone else? Can we even call it luck or chance? Why do some people stack up a fortune while others can barely make money for the next day's meal?

Those questions have been asked a thousand times, never once with a satisfying answer. I realised the problem wasn't the lack of explanation since I always got them to the exact question I asked. The question should be put forward so that the answer can also be complete.

Whether we are just dreaming or searching for the truth in the stories yet unknown in this universe, at some point, all of us will get to know what interests us at least a little.

Therefore, this is the proper question: How does the whole work?

The Questions

Summer of 1996.

As I glared at my computer's monitor, roaming the universe of the Internet, I wondered what a fantastic thing that was. Millions of computers connected through the ether form the invisible empire of the Internet. In mere moments, everything becomes available to everyone who decides to step into this wonderland with their computer. As I signed onto a server in Los Angeles, using Netscape, waiting for the data to download to my computer, a line of thoughts crossed my mind:

That massive amount of information is available in this electric dimension; where are they coming from, and where are they headed? All of the fruits of the millions of people on the net, and what is even more critical, accessible by everyone, so on this endlessly complex World Wide Web, everyone can move wherever they like.

Perhaps as we are only a few years away from the new millennium, we are nearing the solution, perhaps thanks to this technology, we will be able to reach what every person secretly wishes for in their heart. The real question is: will this technological advancement open the doors to our future, or will it destroy mankind as we know it? What does that depend on? How can we control it? Can we even do that, or must we accept that the politicians in leading positions will define our existence even more so than today?

Those questions have been raised multiple times, but only small crumbs of answers came back. I could feel that some missing puzzle pieces needed to be added for this picture to be flawlessly whole.

Once all the data was loaded, I watched a video about a film star. The actress about whom the film was made was born in Australia and since then has moved to the United States and had been enjoying her life with the riches she had. I thought she was in her forties, and her beauty, her movements, her ebony black hair and the kind features of her face enchanted me, nevertheless.

After a few scenes, I watched a reporter talk with her on the round terrace of one of her seaside mansions. The poor audio quality prohibited me from accurately understanding the conversation somewhat. Still, there was a sentence I grasped fully: "The fact that I got where I am today, I can only thank myself for that...".

"Blimey!" I thought. "That was a bold statement."

Most of them would start listing names of people to whom they owe vast chunks of their success, wealth, or fame. Still, she appropriated everything and stated that every bit of her success was hers. Hers only, risking that she might be seen as entitled, selfish or arrogant.

Probably that didn't bother her at the least. She answered every question confidently; she seemed to be the person who knew what she was talking about. Yes. She knew.

I looked at the electric clock on the wall. The second and minute hands stepped from one line onto the other with soft clicks, not caring about anyone or anything, only drawing their circles as if it wasn't even the time they were to show, as if they were only dancing around on the silver-coloured minute and second lines.

Outside, the darkness has engulfed the world, and the three hands of the clock all slowly but indeed neared number twelve.

"It's late", I thought, then exited the world of data and said goodnight to my computer.

In the bathroom, my mind was constantly filled with the thought of the actress. Not only because she was so attractive, even though it could already be enough reason for me to fall asleep with her in my mind, but actually, it was her brave statement I couldn't get out of my head.

Was it true, or did she just want to show off to the reporter?

I've read a lot about people who credited their fame to themselves alone, their vivid creativity, wealth and success, and confidence. I haven't found a reason to doubt these people, though that has never happened to me that way. I have had wishes and goals as much as I can, but until now, I have only reached more minor success; my great goals seem so far and unreachable.

When I returned to my room, I sat in the armchair next to my bed before lying down. This was my favourite place in the flat. I simply called it: the Chair. The bright flame-red cover did not match the walls of my room a bit. The style didn't resonate with the rest of the furniture either. Still, if something was on my mind if I was meditating or had problems to sort out, I always found solace in the comfort of it.

It has seen more of the world than I have. Its cover was slowly wearing off already, but its high headboard and soft, squishy seat satisfied all my needs for comfort, so sometimes I found myself sitting in it for hours, conversing with my thoughts.

I looked out through the window onto the clear summer night sky to say goodnight to my loyal friends, the stars; they wait for me every day, even if not precisely in the same spot in the sky.

Before I lay down to sleep, I wondered a bit about the universe to give myself over to the magic of my dreams. Where does it begin, where is its end, and what happens between the two ends of the spectrum?

I didn't know where to look for the answer, but I longed for that knowledge, which would enable me to give complete and precise answers to every question I had. The one I don't have to prove to anyone, the one I needn't force people to accept and the one from which anyone can feel the air of the entire, unfalsifiable truth.

I lay in my bed and watched the stars for another while. "Sure", I thought, "I would get all the answers if only the stars could talk."

Andem

A pleasant, calm wind touched my body. It caressed me delicately, but then I reached for the blanket, noticing I started to shiver. It was a surprise that I was already covered up to my neck.

My eyes were still closed. I was afraid if I opened them, I'd wake up fully, and I never liked to knock the sleepiness out of my eyes so abruptly. Still, I continued to feel the calm wind on my body, and I thought I must have left my window open for the night. That happened quite often since I didn't have an air-conditioner, and the heat of the summer loved to push its way into my room too. But the air was cold this time, so it might have been raining before.

Thus, I reluctantly opened my eyes and sat up. The window was to the right of my bed, so I could open and close it from a seated position whenever I had to. As always, I stretched my arm out to close the window to keep the cold out, but the process failed since I realised the window was shut.

As I adjusted my blanket, my eyes passed over the Chair near my bed, but it took about two seconds until I realised someone was sitting in my place.

When I discovered I was not alone in the room, I jumped up in fear and ran to the light switch. This reaction probably stuck with me since childhood since my parents used to calm me this way. They said if I was afraid of the bogeyman, I should turn on the lights, and he would disappear and not return.

That always worked.

Not this time.

I turned the switch on, but my heart almost jumped out of its place since what I expected did not actually happen.

This time the bogey stayed in my room, and I saw as... I saw it as it was smiling. Smiling at me kindly and gently. This is when I got my next surprise but far from the last one.

It wasn't a night-time monster; if it was, it wasn't scary. Quite the contrary. I found myself in front of the actress I saw in the Hollywood Report film.

Her beautiful black hair draped over her shoulders; her green eyes showed stunningly on the lamp's light. Her smile was breathtaking, even though I knew she was probably laughing at my blue-dotted pyjamas. My heart's rhythm started normalising; my breath returned to its usual tempo since I realised I was not awake. The whole thing was just a stupid dream. A vivid, lucid dream, perhaps.

Okay, I only thought it was. So, if I am dreaming, nothing terrible can happen to me. And if it is so, I could say something too. I put a childish grin on my face and unconfidently said:

"Hi! How are you?"

She nodded slightly.

"Hm…" she said. "Great."

I was still struck wordless. I wasn't expecting a visitor for the night. I wasn't prepared; I had no idea what to say.

"How are you here?" I finally asked, but I didn't wait for the answer since I remembered that I was dreaming.

"I know", I added quickly, "everything is possible in a dream."

She suddenly stood up from the Chair and took a step towards me.

I didn't know how long it would last but I wished it would never be over. She stood in front of me in that green dress made of light fabric, as if she had stepped out from a beautiful painting or as if I was imagining her. 'What am I thinking? Isn't a lucid dream the way we want it to be?'

The young woman was watching the bookshelf and slowly dragged her finger across all the books she passed.

"You aren't dreaming." She said calmly. "Not right now."

This time I smiled.

"Hm. Of course."

She looked at me, and on her face, I discovered a chilling gravity.

"You really aren't...."

I decided I won't argue with her about that now; whatever that was, it felt good.

"Okay! But how did you get here?" I asked.

"I came to see you." She answered although she didn't about the how part.

"Why?"

"Because you wanted me to."

I found myself boasting the childish grin again. When I saw her on the Internet, it truly did occur to me that I would love to meet her.

"And anyone, who would like to meet an actress can have a date with them at night?" Okay, that came out way differently than I meant it.

"I am not an actress."

"Well yes of course you are. I saw you on a recording yesterday when..."

She didn't let me finish the sentence and said:

"That wasn't me."

I grew a bit unsure.

"No? Then..."

She stepped closer to me.

"My name is Andem," she said after a short break.

That certainly wasn't that actress' name. She, on the other hand, was like a clone of her.

"Excuse me, but I don't understand a word," I said eventually.

"You wanted to understand the way the Whole works, right? So, I came to answer your questions."

Hah! This is great! Until now, I have always wished for this, but now, a dream in the shape of an actress named Andem came to me of all people to answer my questions which to a lot seemed mystical and unanswerable; I couldn't take the situation seriously.

"So that's why?" I asked, still a bit unsure.

Andem turned around and went to the window.

"What do you want, Arsenio?" She asked while she was looking at the quiet life outside.

I was surprised at hearing my name, but I figured I should get used to surprises.

"The truth", I answered, this time more confidently.

She remained silent, which led me to believe she was expecting more of an answer, so I figured I would try better. Why not? Who knows how long we will play this game?

"I want to learn. I want to learn all that helps me live, all that helps me understand people and nature. If there is a method for this, I want to learn how I can control my life, how I can handle adverse events without frustration, or to be able to turn anything into an advantage for myself and I want to learn how I can influence my own fate." These couple sentences truly energised me.

Andem turned back and looked at me.

"I am willing to help you achieve this, but we must talk about something before we begin."

I paid attention to every word she said. I started to feel that something was about to begin, something that would change my life forever.

"I am willing to show you the Whole", she continued, "I will help you understand everything. But! Don't believe in anything, don't believe anything. Ask, but stay far away from the concept of faith, since you will not require it at the least, it would rather limit you in accomplishing your quest for truth. You have to understand, you have to recognise reality and you have to learn everything. You can decide what you want to do right now. Will you learn or will you not learn? Only those two options exist. If you learn, commit to that with all your existence because if you put less energy into learning than you would actually be able to, you will be stuck where you are now and in this case, it was better if you just laid down to wake up tomorrow as the same person you were yesterday. However, if you decide that you will focus all your attention on learning, and you actually do that, you will be able to learn everything and impossible will lose its meaning in your mind."

She fell silent for a couple minutes, letting my brain cells work before she asked the question of a lifetime.

"So? What did you decide?"

Whatever that was, I had a feeling that there was something serious behind all the information I got from my physical senses, something invisible to me. I could sense from Andem's voice that whichever decision I was to make, it would be an important one.

I waited for another couple of seconds and said promptly:

"I will learn."

Law Of Simplicity

She smiled at me again.

"Let's go then," she said, grabbing my hand.

I was still standing there in my pyjamas.

"I can't go like this," I exclaimed, a bit bothered. "First I have to change into something more appropriate for outside."

Andem looked like she didn't understand.

"Why?" she asked.

"What do you mean, why? I cannot step out on the street like this, the whole world will laugh at me."

I saw something like "Oh, you will learn, buddy" on Andem's face, but she left me to it.

"Will this be fine?" she asked, pointing to my night-time wear.

"What?" I asked because I didn't get it.

I didn't understand what she meant, but then I looked at my pyjamas... to be more precise, the clothing which had replaced them. I was speechless. Jeans, trainers, a beige shirt with wide stripes and a denim jacket replaced my nice, blue-dotted pyjamas.

"Let's go," she said, grabbing my hand again.

We started in the direction of the windows, and before I could voice my confusion, we leapt through the glass and the wall without damaging them. We were rising higher and higher. I saw the whole street, the city, and everything suddenly disappeared.

At first, I thought we wouldn't stop until the stars, but suddenly, we found ourselves on a hillside filled with thousand-coloured flowers, and the Sun shone in our faces.

An incomparably beautiful scene unfolded in front of our eyes.

We saw a forest in the distance; behind our backs was an untouched-looking field of flowers that seemed like no human or animal had ever walked across. I didn't see any sign of human presence or settlements either.

Andem let go of my hand, sat on the grass and indicated that I should sit beside her. The air was fresh, clean and could only exist in places far from civilisation. I inhaled the aromatic scent deeply and felt it coursing through my body.

"Divine," I said. Then I turned to Andem. "It is a shame this all only exist in my dreams."

Andem picked a flower and inhaled its scent.

"I have already told you." She stated calmly. "You aren't dreaming now."

Her statement was laughable, at the least.

"What do you mean it isn't a dream?" I asked. "This can't be reality!"

While playing with the flower, she turned her face towards me. Her eyes glinted in the sunlight.

"Why not?"

"Why?! Because we flew, because we went through a wall and because you conjured me some clothing. That kind of stuff don't happen."

She reacted to my statement with silence at first, then asked:

"Arsenio. Are you familiar with reality?"

"How could I not be?"

"Are you sure?"

I wanted to answer immediately, but then I thought for a moment. Do I really know it? Then what is it that I want to learn?

I panned the area with my eyes.

"This place seems to be real," I said, becoming a bit unsure.

"Why does it only "seem to be"?"

I stood up and took a few steps down the hill. After a few meters, I stopped, bent down and picked a white flower with many petals.

I turned around and started going back.

"I don't understand this," I said finally.

"But it is simple." She said while also standing up. "Everything that is happening to you is real, the true freedom, limitless opportunities…"

She stepped over to me and put her hand on my shoulder.

"What you think of as dreams are all completely real. The past, the present and the future."

"If dreams are also reality…"

She cut in again before I could finish my sentence.

"No. Only the dreams are reality."

I was a bit dumbstruck by what I heard. I always tended to be impatient, and this tendency was slowly taking over me again.

"Okay, but then what the hell is that I live in?" I asked with a tiny bit of frustration. "The everyday things I do, the things that surround me, that are parts of my life. What are those? "

Andem, spellbound by the beauty, was bathing in the sunshine. She threw her arms apart again and danced like a young girl in the field of flowers.

"What do you think they are?" she asked.

"Are you trying to tell me that all those are dreams?"

She stopped dancing and looked at me.

"You learn fast." She said, smiling. "The Whole is nothing but imagination, illusion, fantasy. The fruit of your mind."

I broke out in laughter. Maybe I couldn't think of any other way of reacting to the fact that she uttered her last words simply as if she was telling a hilarious joke.

Andem didn't take offence. It took me a couple of seconds to stop myself, which was also enough time to realise how childish my behaviour was. I felt embarrassed.

"Forgive me!" I said.

"I am not mad at you. I didn't expect anything else."

A short silence followed, and she retook hold of my hand.

"Before I start to explain anything to you," I felt some superhuman calmness in her voice, "remember, everything is a lot simpler than you think. That is the Law of Simplicity. If you ever come across a problem and you search for a solution, or you are just entertained by some idea, don't overcomplicate anything, because nothing is as complicated as it seems. Always search for answer in the simplicity of things, and you shall find it."

She let go of my hand, but I continued to feel her soft touch. Her gaze was fixed on me in an examining manner.

"If everything was so simple, I would know the explanation for everything," I smelled my flower "and every arisen problem could have been solved easily, right?"

She slowly started to walk down the hill. I rushed to catch up with her then we walked beside each other on the green grass in the field of colourful flowers.

"Ever since you were a small child, your teachers and parents all taught it to you," it was as if every vibration of her voice was caressing my ears, "how complicated the world is, that you can only make a living in this world if you finish the schools you are supposed to attend and learned the things a couple of leaders of some commission decided you should learn, together with some people who are considered to be really smart, who were named scientists and thought certain things work a certain way. They experienced their revelations as their own and then used logical arguments to make other people also believe things work the way they discovered."

She took a small break. Perhaps she told me more efficiently to allow me to process all the information.

"Just think about it", she continued silently. "Through your history, which you also learned at school, how many crazy and laughable ideas have been believed to be reality? How many lives have been taken in the name of God or love instead of trusting in clear thought and wisdom when someone considered things didn't work the way some leaders and priests believed they did? People haven't changed ever since. Though the world has become more civilised and the fast-technological developments made people think they are closer to the truth, they are only further away."

"The schools and parents are doing the same thing now as religion did back then: they are forcing their beliefs and perspectives onto the children. Of course, I wouldn't for a second think that it is ill will guide them to do that; I am sure they have good intentions, but they are completely limiting people's freedom this way."

"Freedom is achieved when you can do whatever you want. If you want to buy yourself an aeroplane or if you want to have a good meal in a fancy and expensive restaurant, you should be able to do that without financial or moral restrictions. The textbooks, your parents, teachers, TV and newspapers all coded it inside you that life is complicated, and nothing works simply. But oh yes, everything does."

I listened to every single word she said in silence, and I felt like she brought up the deepest yet unspoken thoughts from my mind just now. Suppose I only looked back to childhood stories and books when we only learned to read in elementary school, where they portrayed poverty as a positive value and wealth as an evil characteristic. In that case, the things Andem was telling me were starting to make sense. Laws were created by people, suppressing all the urges of mankind to be free. The Bible, Quran, Tora, and all the religious books contained all the strict rules and laws God bestowed upon us, telling us what we aren't allowed to do. But they all had been written by humans as well.

"For centuries then," I started, staring at the flower in my hands, "we have been living in a lie. But then what is the truth and what is the evidence that it really is the truth?"

Andem answered as calmly as she had been all this time:

"The fact that you are searching for evidence limits your imagination and your knowledge. Your studies have planted a type of belief inside you, thanks to which you wrongly judge reality. You demand so-called evidence and facts only because you are so stuck to your wrong thoughts, and you state that if you get what you ask from me, you might change the picture in your head. However, you might also proclaim me as a liar and a fraud because you don't believe your eyes, feelings or simplicity; you only believe in the education planted in you through the years. The media and public news sources give you a clear picture of what you should think. The people in power always create specific images in people's minds to influence them."

"It is like living in a room with no idea about what it feels like to be outside of it. You enclose yourself within four walls with no windows because people who think they are smarter than you think you are safe this way. They inform you about what happens on the outside. You believe that without any questions, they will paint the picture of the outside world exactly the way they want it to look, regardless of the truth. If possible, the goal is to keep you inside the room without you even wanting to step out. That is precisely what you should be doing. Opening the door and learning the scent of fresh air, the true feeling of freedom, that beautiful world you couldn't even imagine before because you were taught something different. Therefore, I said at first that you should delete all faith and beliefs from your mind since they significantly inhibit your ability to learn and attain free knowledge. You will search for evidence due to your wrong belief system, and this time you will get it once you realise how simple everything is. The evidence is deep inside you, inside the truth itself."

It was no question she knew how to argue.

"You said that my dreams are the reality, and what I perceive to be reality is actually…"

"Not more than illusions, ideas and wrong beliefs forced upon you by misinformed or manipulative people."

Even though she seemed likeable, I had trouble processing the things she mentioned.

"But what is the truth?" I asked impatiently.

Andem let the silence sort out some of the chaos inside my head, created by the previous information flood.

"What is your favourite car brand?" she asked.

I didn't need much time to think about that:

"Jaguar."

"Now think for a while then tell me, what do you think would be the simplest way for you to get a car like that?"

I didn't understand why she told me to think about that since I only knew about a straightforward method.

"Purchasing it." I shrugged.

"How much does a Jaguar cost?" She asked.

"Oh well... a lot of money."

"Do you have the money?"

"No. I don't have that much money."

I started to understand what she was getting at.

"Okay, so can I choose from every possibility?" I had to ask for clarification more often than less since I met her.

She nodded.

"I don't have to take the law into consideration?"

"Most definitely don't."

I chuckled. Was she planning to make me a villain of sorts?

"Then I can break into an auto salon and steal one," I smirked.

"There is an even simpler way." She smiled.

Hm... I really had to think about this one.

"I can win a lot of money on the lottery." I blurted out after a while.

She stopped and sat down in the grass.

"Okay. I will wait for that."

I had to acknowledge that whatever this game's name was, she was playing it well. Seems like that also wasn't the simplest solution. There was no way I could figure out the answer.

Andem indicated that I should sit down beside her.

"See," she said kindly. "You overcomplicate everything as much as you can when it actually isn't more difficult than turning on your computer, only now you have been on the verge of getting to the answer multiple times. It is in front of your eyes, but you can't see it."

I gave up.

"Okay, what is the solution then?"

"You will realise that yourself. But now..." She stood up and grabbed my hands. "It is best if we start everything from the beginning."

The field, the flowers, the blue sky, the sunshine, everything that surrounded us a minute ago disappeared suddenly. "Wow!" I thought, "Worlds are disappearing from around me and I am supposed to acknowledge that it isn't just a dream?"

Free Will

We stood in a big room which looked like a NASA control centre. There were desks next to one another everywhere, computers, monitors and keyboards filling the desktops. There must have been at least 40 computers, probably more. All were facing in the same direction; the desks and chairs were aligned so that everyone could comfortably see the massive monitor in the front of the room, which was a couple meters wide. I presumed that the contents of any single computer could be projected onto this big screen.

Andem stepped to one of the computers and sat down. I examined the other computers for a while, walked around the room between the desks and noted that the machines probably weren't old. There were nicely packed stacks of papers next to the computers on each desk. I picked up a couple pieces of paper to see what their contents were, but I found that they were all blank, white paper sheets.

I walked back to Andem and sat down next to her.

She turned to me.

"How much time do you think has passed since we left your home?" she asked.

"I am not sure… About an hour I'd say."

"Wrong. Not a minute has passed since then."

My eyes became round and wide like saucers.

"How come?"

"The thing you call time doesn't exist."

Now that exceeded all my comprehension capacities. Andem might have been right, and my inability to comprehend such ideas stemmed from years of education and social conditioning. Still, whatever the cause was, these things seemed extraordinary to me.

"If there is no time," I asked, "how could I have grown up, how could I have been born at all, how can I travel, how can I study and improve, how can I do anything at all?"

She flipped a switch next to the desk, and in the following moment, all computers were turned on.

"It is all like the Internet," she said, typing something on the keyboard. "What do you do, when you are searching for something? For example, information about one of Ireland's theme parks?"

"I connect to an Irish server, then find one of the databases that lists links to content related to theme parks and their locations and then I'll pick the one I was looking for and read the details about it."

"How long does it take to find this information?"

"That depends on some things. Sometimes it takes a couple seconds, sometimes an hour or longer."

"And because of that, you believe that time exists, right?"

"Yes of course, how could I do anything otherwise? Everything would stop."

"Well, not really."

She was working on the computer, and a list appeared on the monitor.

"Look!" she said, pointing to the rows of references under one another. "Here are all the theme parks, their names and addresses, and all information about them."

"Yes, I can see that," I assured.

"This information was there long before you even started searching for it. All of it has been there."

"I get it, but what does it have to do with the non-existence of time?"

Andem could see that I was one of the slower types.

"Calculate the following and pay attention to how long it will take you."

"Sure."

"Twenty-three multiplied by twelve."

I was never good at that in my head, not to mention that pocket calculators are a must-have, which, of course, I didn't have on me courtesy of magical outfit change before we left, so it took me a while, but I managed to get the answer.

"Two hundred and seventy-six," I answered proudly since it was fast compared to my usual speed. "Took about ten, fifteen seconds."

"So, let's say it took you ten seconds. For someone else, it would take five, for another thirty. However, the answer was already there. Always has been."

She fell silent after this. I felt like I just discovered the most incredible realisation in my life, which filled me with a fantastic feeling and frightened me simultaneously. Andem waited calmly until I organised my thoughts back together. The enlightening feeling stunned me, but I kept my composure somewhat.

"So…" I could barely put my thoughts into words, "all solutions to all problems arising in life are always and constantly, statically there, not moving forward or backwards, simply existing?"

"Exactly. There is no past or future. There is only present."

We were both smiling, and that was for the same reason: I understood.

Andem leaned back in her chair and looked at me with a satisfied expression. However, she knew this was only the beginning for me.

"You learned the most important thing," she said. "This is what everything is based on, all you have mentioned; birth, learning, improvement, success, failure, illness and death as well."

She typed something into the computer again, which resulted in an image appearing on the large screen, portraying a grid with many intersections and directions. Looking at the infinite, tangled lines, it looked more like a spatial spider-web than a grid. My first association was the massive World Wide Web of the Internet as if I was looking at hundreds or thousands of computers and servers connected to one another.

Andem left me to examine the web for a while before she spoke.

"What you see here is your life."

"Hm… It is quite a mass," I said, somewhat cynical. "So much for simplicity."

Andem didn't react to my provocative tone.

"It truly is simple. You understand that everything is already there at once, so no change occurs; nothing passes away; it only seems like it."

"Every point of intersection on this massive web is another variation of opportunities. There are unfathomably many of them. Infinite. The lines connecting them show their relevance and connection to each other. On this monitor, you can see the past, the present and the future. Every intersection is a possible version of a moment. Imagine that every point was a link to another computer, and you could freely move between them. Let's say now you are on a computer's informational database. Suppose you decide anything in case of a failure or problem concerning anything in your life. In that case, all you do is step over to another dot and experience it. You feel as if you are experiencing it now, like when you search the database of a computer far away or use it for any other purpose.

I was paying attention to every word she said.

"The goal is to understand that instead of time there is a mechanism at play which gives the feeling of change to comprehend that mechanism which is what you call time."

I tried to satisfy her expectations.

"On the Internet, I can step from any single computer onto another one and can use it to my will, of course following certain rules. The changes happening in real-life work the same way?"

"It closely resembles it, yes. With the difference that there is no change in space or time, and you define your own limits and rules. You don't have a past or a future. You have the present, which is all there is. Out of the endless opportunities presented to you on a tray, you can choose whichever one you like. All opportunities and possibilities are there, you just must decide which one you want. What do you want in life? Wealth and happiness or poverty and stress?"

I had a confident answer to this question, but it was probably the same one that anyone else would say.

"I want to be rich and happy."

"When I phrased the question, both opportunities were already in existence and they are right now as well. So, you just chose the first one. You don't have to do anything else, but: Decide."

All of that seemed so far away, unimaginable, unbelievably simple, and I couldn't make these thoughts my own. However, they stood a lot closer to my heart than the ones I learned at school or from everyone else, for that matter. So, my future or my perceived future can be anything. Everything is true; everything can happen; I just must choose which option I want. Okay, but how?

"How is this possible?" I asked, a bit more excited. "I mean in practice, how does this work?"

Andem was more kind and patient with me than any other person has ever been.

"What is the difference between theory and practice then?" her voice calmed me.

"Theory is something" I started my answer, "which we think of, we make up, in here." I pointed to my head.

Andem was quietly paying attention to me.

"And practice is" I continued, "what we do, what we accomplish in the physical world..."

The Sun suddenly started shining in my mind, sunshine flowed through my brain cells, and my eyes glistened like a 3-year-old kid's when their parents placed the birthday cake with three candles in front of them.

"Blimey! You aren't trying to say that it is truly possible for us to think of something and that is enough for it to actually happen, right?"

Andem indicated with a beautiful smile that I hit the bullseye.

"I didn't say it, you did."

"So, I can just think of something and it will happen?" I repeated the question.

My leader nodded.

"But how?"

"You just said it. You only need to imagine it."

I stood up and started walking between the desks.

"Andem, I have already imagined so many things in my life and yet, none of them happened, I didn't get what I wanted. They remained fantasies, dreams, wishes."

"That, what you have imagined actually has happened. It's there. Always has been. You only didn't accept it; your limits didn't let the power of your conscience create change. Your belief attained throughout the years is what prevented you from achieving that. Whatever you were wishing for, you didn't imagine it the way you really wanted it, what you thought and believed was reality hid in the background somewhere and you unwillingly stuck to it."

She saw that I didn't understand a word. How could I possibly be stuck to something that I want to change? She gestured for me to step closer and then conjured a deck of cards from nowhere. She fanned them out and extended her arm towards me, holding the cards with their colours facing up.

"Pick a card," she said.

I chose the nine of Spades.

"So, the nine of Spades it is," she closed the deck. "Place it on the table here with its back facing down."

I placed it down, face up.

"Now tell me, which card would you like to change it to?" she played with the cards with the skill of a sleight-of-hand artist.

"To the Ace of Spades," I answered.

Andem took the card out of the deck and placed it face up onto the previous one to completely cover the other card.

"Which card do you see?"

"The Ace of Spades."

"And which one is on the table?"

"The Ace of Spades and the Nine of Spades."

"Exactly. So, you know that the previous card is on the table, regardless of the second card of your choice."

It happened more often that I didn't understand what she was saying.

"But of course, if it is there, I obviously know that it is," I said.

"There is no difference between consciousness or awareness and imagination."

She picked up the Ace of Spades. To my surprise, the nine of Spades were nowhere to be found.

"Can you see the first card now?" she said, pointing to where the cards were.

"No. I can't see it."

"So, you know it is not there, right?"

"Of course."

"But you are only imagining it."

I couldn't say anything; I decided to wait for her to clarify the picture.

"You know something if you have seen it, experienced it, felt it, but you only see, feel and experience something once you know it. Your awareness is your imagination and your imagination is your awareness."

"Everything that surrounds you in the world: the walls of your room, the furniture, your computer, your city, they all exist in your own world. You are only imagining it. It is all just an illusion. And as it is an illusion, you can do with it as you please, you use it however you like. You can call it a miracle if it suits you better."

"Furthermore, the fact that most of the people see the world as nearly the same for everyone is because they surrender to their emotions, fear, their eyes and their external senses but not their minds."

I was still listening quietly. I just couldn't comprehend yet what she was saying.

"Faith, imagination, awareness and knowledge are all the same things", she continued, "Illusion, magic. And time is something you imagine since everything exists already; things don't pop into existence in every following moment. Your emotions are also imagined since regret, hate, and pain don't exist. There are only two things in total: love and knowledge."

My head felt like it would explode from everything I just heard.

"Let's see if I understand correctly." I started my summary. "Everything that was is and will be already in existence."

Andem nodded.

"So," I said, running my fingers through my hair. "Time is a completely pointless and non-existent factor. Any step I take has already been worked out, I only live the moment with my emotions, fear, pain, joy, stress and all, but what I experience is just my brainchild. So, I am making it up."

I took a short break. This time Andem didn't react in any way.

"If I create everything that surrounds me, then the things I think of and the events I am experiencing are created by me at that very moment, which already disproves the previously mentioned hypothesis."

Andem stepped to the big monitor and pointed to the web.

"Your imagination is just a navigator on this web.," she said, dragging her finger from one point to another. "At this point, you don't have a Jaguar, at this other point you can go ahead and sit inside it to enjoy its comfort." She then moved her hand to another point. "While here, you are playing your guitar in a subway, begging for money."

I shuddered at the thought. "What is this woman talking about?" I thought. How I play my guitar would probably leave me starving to death.

"With your imagination, you only choose one of the many options", she continued. "And the many choices you make one after another is what your concept of time actually is. According to your current knowledge, faith or imagination, right now, you cannot get anything from one moment to the other, let alone such an expensive car, since according to your education, this is physically impossible, and you navigate yourself to the points where you work a lot and fight for the money and everything else which brings you closer to your goal little by little, and once you will arrive at the point where you could've gotten a lot simpler, without all the tiring work and that long unnecessary bypass."

She smiled mischievously.

"I would rather not go into details with the latter version," she remarked kindly, then continued with her presentation.

"However, if you wish for something and imagine it if you want to create, navigating with the power of your mind on the net, then in order for change to occur, you need to step away from one point to be able to step onto another one. When you are just daydreaming, fantasising about a certain wish of yours, it is like your right foot is already on that dot, but due to your indoctrinated mind, you cannot fully move onto it, you feel like you are stuck on the previous spot with the left foot still there. If you want to move effortlessly on this grid, the first thing you need to rid yourself of are your current beliefs."

She stopped for a while, then continued.

"Until now, the reason you experienced time and the reason you though everything that you made up or built only came into existence then and there, because you have always lived your life in only one dimension, and you only experienced that given small fraction of the Whole, and at that moment you weren't familiar with all the other options that were, are and always will be available to you."

I started to understand the correlations and realised how simple everything indeed was. With the help of this knowledge, all problems, stress, fear and anxiety are substituted by happiness and a simple, uncomplicated life. I just have to live with the opportunities.

I smiled as I felt my soul filling up with a calm, pleasant feeling.

"I think I am starting to get it," I said finally. "I myself choose which option I want, and this process is a lot simpler than I thought it was. This is really like magic. I have been always taught that this was impossible, that such doesn't exist, but it seems just like addition and multiplication can be learned, so can this, and by anyone. Even me."

I remembered something.

"I am starting to understand what you said at the beginning of our endeavours. The part where you said that dreams are reality. So, anything I dream at night actually happens and I experience it just like real life."

"Yes. When you sleep, all your limits and previous beliefs disappear without you being aware of it, and your true self wanders around on the web of possibilities. This self tries these opportunities and, in that dimension, everything you dream actually happens."

She took a short break. This time almost everything she said was clear to me.

"And while this is going on, what happens with me?" I asked.

"No change happens, since the options on the web of possibilities are chosen independently from time and space, so in your dreams and the events you experience, the passing of time is just an illusion. Everything takes place in one moment. You don't remember every one of your night-time experiences. You go through a lot more than could fit in a few hours of sleep. The more important parts are usually the only ones you remember when you start living by your limits again. Out of the many experienced possibilities, you touch on a couple in the world of your beliefs too."

Yet again, I realised the reason for an occurrence I hadn't understood before.

"So, this is the reason why sometimes I feel like I have lived through a given experience already?"

Andem nodded.

"And anything that you are able to do while dreaming can be done anytime, everything that happens in your dreams have happened, is happening, will happen and the illusions you have experienced and felt while living what you thought is the only reality when you were awake, can also be changed to your wish if you only let go of your limits."

A strong urge took hold of me suddenly.

"Please, teach me how to do it!"

"You will learn everything. You will learn the Whole, but as I mentioned before, you will have to be the one who uses it, I cannot help you with that. Every possibility is already existent, you just have to choose which one you want the most."

I stopped to think for a second. The things inside my head started to clear, but something bothered my brain.

"But if every problem is already solved, if every solution is already created, then there is nothing left to invent, nothing left to solve, and thus what is the point of us living at all?"

Andem stepped toward me, and I felt we would be leaving for another place again. She stood in front of me and touched my shoulder as she answered.

"Learning."

The Lesson

She made everything vanish again, the computers, the furniture, the big monitor, and everything else. A city appeared before us as we were slowly surrounded by buildings, streets and pavements. The place looked familiar. After orienting myself, I realised that we were standing in front of one of a vast shopping mall.

There were a lot of people around. At first, I thought we were just objective spectators of the events, but then I realised we were a part of whatever was going to happen. Andem touched my shoulder and, with her head, indicated towards a young lady conversing with another woman. Her daughter was standing next to her, observing the people around her. She couldn't be more than 5 years old.

"Now," Andem started, "watch the little girl but don't do anything."

She looked deep into my eyes as if she were to force her statement into my brain.

"Whatever happens, do not do anything. Do you understand?"

I nodded silently, then directed my attention at the child. She held a long-eared, soft, white bunny plush in her hands. Her blonde hair was neatly tied with some cute, colourful band. She was a sweet creature and was awed by the bustle of everyday life, the huge buildings and the colourful cars. Her mom talked to the other woman as if she had forgotten about her daughter completely. Maybe it was a friend she hadn't seen for a long time. The little girl noticed a tiny dog running around between the legs of the people with its tongue out, barking randomly.

The next moment, the girl ran after the dog without the mother or the friend noticing. They were preoccupied with talking about the dealings of their lives. The dog thought it had enough of racing around people's legs, so it decided to cross to the other side of the street, which wasn't so busy with pedestrians. It didn't care much about the passing cars.

I had a bad feeling. I wanted to shout to the mother: "Hey miss, pay a bit more attention to your offspring, will you?" but then I remembered Andem's warning and decided to silently watch the events unfold.

The girl ran after the dog; she wouldn't stop until she petted the tiny creature. The four-legged little being wasn't only furry but also was moving, a combination that excited the little child's mind; a moving, furry thing got to pet. Her mother noticed nothing of this; her attention was only taken from the conversation by the horrible screeching of the brakes of a silver BMW.

I shouted at the exact moment as the mother.

"No!"

Suddenly everything disappeared, and we were back in the computer-filled room. I couldn't see what happened. A huge question mark shone on my face as I looked at Andem.

She again stepped to the monitor displaying the web.

"What happened, Arsenio?" she asked, pointing to one of the dots. "Let's assume, this is the point the little girl's life started from", she pointed to another dot, "and this is where we stepped out of the picture. What could have happened?"

The storm of feelings this event caused started to calm down.

"I think a lot of things could have happened. We cannot know for sure what happened after everything disappeared."

"What do you think, did the girl know what was going to happen?"

"How could has she known? She wouldn't have run off of the sidewalk then."

"Why? What have should she known for her not to step onto the road?"

"Well, that she could get hit by a car."

I considered my answer completely straightforward, but as Andem looked at me questioningly, I realised I should change my statement.

"So, it didn't even occur to her that she could get hurt?" I managed to turn it into a question.

I felt some sort of relief.

"So, the girl didn't get hurt then?" I asked with hope.

Andem didn't say a word; she just stepped over to the keyboard, typed in some commands and the place we had just been to appear on the big screen.

I saw the dog run out onto the street, and immediately after it, the girl. The driver of the silver BMW saw the animal and braked but realised he didn't have enough space to stop and turned the wheel to avoid hitting the dog. It was too late for him to recognise that a small girl was running after the dog. The car hit the girl, whose body was thrown into the air. Her limp body landed a couple meters away. My heart almost broke at the sight. Within a couple of seconds, there was a big chaos; the mother of the small girl cried and screamed in despair, hugging the body of her dead child...

Slowly the video disappeared from the monitor, and the web appeared again. I felt such an intense pain in my stomach as possibly ever. My throat felt dry, and I tried to swallow but failed. I only saw the girl for a few minutes, but I grew so attached as if I had known her since birth, and now she was the victim of a stupid accident...

I looked at Andem with sad eyes and saw she expressed no emotion. It was the same kind, soft face, without any sign of pain or sadness.

"Why?" I asked with my voice being weak. "Why did it have to be that way?"

Andem hugged me to provide some comfort. She knew she knew for sure that the story of the small girl shook me terribly, but what was her goal with it? The hug filled my soul with such calmness as if nothing terrible had ever happened, which would have thrown me out of my otherwise rarely stable emotional balance.

She let go of me and then looked me in my eyes.

"It didn't have to," she said, with such love and goodness in her voice that only exists in a mother speaking to her child or as loving siblings talk to each other. Again, she stepped to the keyboard and started the previous video. I didn't want to watch it again, but I hoped she was showing it to me again because she wanted to explain something.

I saw the girl running after the dog. Brakes screeched, then a loud slam. The BMW braked and pulled the car away, but this time in the other direction, hitting another vehicle. The girl's mother ran desperately to her child, who couldn't even process what had happened and picked her up, hugging her tightly. The driver jumped out of his car and ran over to them.

"Is she okay?" he asked, his voice shaking from fright.

The mother was trying to hold her tears back, unsuccessfully. It was visible on her face that she had thought, "what if...?". She took her child back to the sidewalk without a word.

The picture disappeared from sight again, and Andem and I looked at each other silently. We stood mute for a while before I could utter my first sentence.

"What was that?" I asked dumbly.

Andem made the web appear again on the monitor.

"What we saw at first," she started quietly, "is nothing but your choice out of the opportunities. What we saw the second time was mine. The fact that the roads are dangerous and that anyone who steps out onto them is in danger because of the cars and is likely to get hit and probably die has been in you as a belief, as a part of your consciousness. According to my decision, everybody lives, even the dog, and aside from a great deal of fright and some material damage, nothing bad happens."

"You conjured the creation of your own imagination," she continued," and I did mine. The mom did her own. Do you understand? Probably you and the mother experienced the same thing since none of you would think you could've controlled your illusion; you didn't know you could freely choose from an infinite amount of options and variations, and neither did you see how you could do that."

"I know how to do it, but you and many other people are stuck with your limitations due to the experience you've gained over the years. You will also learn that death as a concept is pointless, too, since – though we do not know what the little girl chose – what you call death is simply a switch from one dimension to another, which everyone has the right to choose. It is the same as deciding whether to go to the cinema or the theatre. You can choose either, and nobody will cry for you if you choose the cinema."

"Thus, the sadness and the crying at funerals are pointless too; it is useless and only indicate the lack of knowledge; since the person who passed away is still alive, they are only improving their knowledge elsewhere."

"Pure love doesn't mean we should grieve for the person who we lost; quite the contrary, it means we respect, celebrate it and let them go with a calm, clean heart, letting go of all the emotional bonds connecting us to them, which are limiting their personal freedom."

"If all people someday would learn what I already know, what you are learning right now, the day would come when everyone could consciously create their own world and personal dimension."

"That is where the Whole will again be made up of pure harmony. People create their own worlds by moving to their choice of a point on the web."

"Still, the problem is that the majority, like sheep, follow the few options and possibilities promoted by your society's leaders."

"Since that is what most people are ever familiar with, it seems to most of them as if there was only one world and no room for decision-making, which is why so many men and women worldwide fight constantly. Knowledge never would create wars and violence. Ignorance, however,... People are not making their own minds but following others'."

I had nothing to ask or comment at this point, so I let her speak while processing everything she said as fast as I could.

"Everybody lives in their own either accepted or rejected lives or they live in their controlled and happy one, regardless, everyone improves and learns. Yes, everybody always develops their knowledge one way or another. The mother definitely learned a lesson from what happened – though we have no idea what she chose, whatever it was, it contained a lesson for her."

She took a slight pause. Then she asked:

"What did you learn, Arsenio?"

"What have I learned?" I scratched my head, not because it was itching, but just because I felt like it. "Maybe that I should not believe what I see, feel or experience, I should only be sure of what I know. Until now I was always under the control of my own ideas, from now on, I want to control them."

Andem's eyes were shining.

"I am proud of you, Arsenio," she said, holding my hand. "And now it is time for you to know the actual reason why everything works, the thing that we both are. I will show you what it is we also are a part of, you and me too: The Cosmic Whole."

Everything started to fade away around us, and I knew: I was about to get the answer to the most critical questions in life.

The Law Of Wholeness

We were standing on the thousand-coloured, flowery hill again. The fresh smell of nature washed through my lungs, and I felt light and calm. The Sun shone just like it had the last time we were here. Everything was bathed in sunshine. Although I knew: that was also only an illusion, and it still had me under control, I felt free. Freer than ever.

Andem sat on the grass. I felt she liked the place and the beautiful feelings with it, the sunshine, the flowers and the smell of nature. I sat down next to her.

We sat next to each other in silence. I closed my eyes; I wanted to feel everything, all that surrounded me; I wanted to feel the presence of Andem too. She pulled her knees up, locked her arms around them and laid her head on her knees, looking at me. In normal circumstances, I would have immediately fallen in love with her, but this wasn't such a moment; there was no love or a bond connecting me to her, yet I still felt something untouchable, which made it seem like we belonged together. She and I.

She stood up suddenly and started to walk up the hill. I followed her for a while with my gaze, then stood up and caught up with her. When we reached the top, she closed her eyes, smiled into the Sun, enjoying the shine, and then looked at me with her beautiful eyes.

"You learned physics in school" She spread her arms wide open, and while talking to me, she kept playing with the magic of the sunshine. "They taught you that there are solid, liquid and gas states of matter. You learned that there are objects and living beings, that energy is just a factor appearing in our everyday lives, that you can use it for heating or lighting, empowering things."

She spun in the light, then turned to me again.

"But did they ever teach you," her face turned solemn, "that everything that you see, you feel, and what surrounds you, within you, of you, by you are all just energy?"

I have gotten to the level where nothing surprised me, but what she said still seemed somewhat weird. Maybe this was still the result of years of my indoctrination.

"How... do you mean that?" I asked uncertainly.

"As I say it. You and I are both energies."

I went silent, not because of the lack of understanding, but because that information shed light on many different things and answered many of my questions. In fact, it made everything Andem taught me so far a lot more digestible. I tried to fit together all the puzzle parts scattered in my brain, but something was still incomplete.

I thought I would get the complete picture if I waited a bit.

"The furniture in your room, the desks, the chairs, the wall, the computer are all just energies, and what's more, they are all the same type of energy. Your thoughts, your voice, the lights, your knowledge is also the same as everything else."

I stared blankly for a few seconds, then returned to the moment.

"As everything until now, this also must have an explanation to it," I said then, "so please tell me how can it be, that a glass of water and a glass of plum brandy are made of the same energy, but one of them hydrates while the other, presuming I can even swallow it, burns my gut?"

"Simple.", she said. "It is, just as anything else, an illusion. You imagine water and brandy to be the way they are. If you transform that image and the experience of the two drinks, water can be as fiery as plum brandy and brandy can be as refreshing as water. In truth, all energy is the same because they make up parts of the Whole…"

I raised my hand, signalling for her to stop, because at that moment – as if I had woken up from a long-lasting coma – something changed inside me. I didn't yet know what it was.

"Let's see, if I understand it..." I said. "There is a big sandbox. I sit in the middle and start building using my little plastic shovel and a small bucket. I make a castle, then a tunnel, then I create a pyramid. All different objects, but they are all made of the same material. Sand. If I decide to do so, I can destroy any one of them, rebuild or transform them. Out of the sand, I create whatever I like, I use it for whatever I want, the sand remains sand, and the quantity and quality or any other attributes of each particle doesn't change, they only form what I create with them. None of the grains of sand disappear or change. The particles of sand aren't anything on their own, not unless I make something with them."

Andem was smiling.

"Congratulations, Arsenio. I think you know everything now. You have passed your exam."

I felt no excitement, enlightenment, happiness or sadness; I felt something constant, confident, stable, calm, yet empowered.

"Okay. This means that when I go home, I can change anything in my surroundings, whatever I like? In truth, I can look at my environment, may that be an object or a living being, as one with myself?"

Andem nodded.

"You already feel one with everything. Since we have returned to this field, you have consciously worked slowly towards being one with everything."

"So, what I am feeling is…"

"You don't feel that. In the Whole," she continued, "you and I make one. Furthermore, this field, our thoughts and we all create one Whole, without feelings."

I listened for a while, and looking into myself, I realised that I learned the truth. No doubt or question formed inside me since I knew I could find all the answers immediately.

"Andem," I said quietly. "Everything you have shown, explained, taught me so far has completely changed the way I view the universe and I don't just think differently about my life, my emotions have also transformed as if they were non-existent."

I searched for words while pausing for a bit. Earlier, I would have become excited when realising something I hadn't known before or frustrated or confused if I didn't understand something; I would have been filled with unease about the uncertainty of my life, I would have been able to love someone, blinded by the fire of the feeling, but now, something I have never yet experienced has taken control over me.

"I don't even know how to say this, how it is possible to express this... I can only say that I am completely calm, but I know this is way more than that. As if I didn't have feelings, as if I wasn't able to be sad or happy about anything, but I don't even miss those feelings. I can clearly see that everything is given, I see the Whole, the true, only reality."

Andem just smiled. She didn't say a word, just gently held my hand. Her touch on my skin wasn't a good or bad feeling anymore; I knew it had happened.

Then suddenly, the flowers and the hill disappeared, and we were standing in a cloudy white, actually not white, in an undetermined coloured something.

"Whatever we are in now," I thought Andem was a couple steps away from me, but I wasn't sure. "It is an illusion just like the ones you have seen so far. You cannot see or feel the true reality since it doesn't exist. Reality is simply nothing and everything, at once."

I looked around again, paying more attention to the details. I only saw this visible-invisible material surrounding us, and I saw this fog-like thing to be so close that I could touch it and indeterminably far away simultaneously. Space became impalpable, just like time.

I saw Andem, and I didn't. I didn't manage to feel her presence as I did on the field or in the computer room; I just knew she was with me.

"Where we are now is the Unity that created everything. The true Whole. We are parts of this, just like all that is visible on the web I showed you on the monitor."

I signalled with just a thought that I wanted to continue.

"This is all that we are" My confidence grew proportionate to my knowledge. "What created the past, the present and the future, and all the dots on the web. This Unity doesn't do anything; it only exists and lets us use all its parts for whatever we want."

Andem's and my knowledge was one already, but she still asked, may be out of custom:

"And why does it do that?"

"To learn, to extend and grow its knowledge. The knowledge that is infinite." I continued. "Love is infinite. Those are the two things it needs, in some way: this is how it feels good and since both are infinite, it constantly tries to acquire more of it. Through us. Thus, I could also state it this way: we acquire it, or I acquire it."

The personal pronouns, everything they thought in school, and the things I learned throughout my life all seemed to lose meaning. My desire for money and the Jaguar has vanished, all of which were the engines behind my life. I knew only three things, but with them everything: Myself, Love and Knowledge…"

Andem was standing next to me and was watching me. She didn't say a word; we understood each other. We didn't ask anything from one another anymore since there was no one another left; it was only the true, the real Me.

Oneness

Suddenly everything inside and around me dissolved. I was surrounded by nothing but light... here and now, I knew that what hadn't even begun had already started. I knew forever... I was one with everything!

Embraced by love and embraced by the light.

Together, Andem, the Universe and I.

I am one with you; I'm one with all.

I love as one with the unknown.

No dream awaits me nor awakening.

There is no more pain, no more suffering.

I am a thought, nothing else.

Not bothered by the future, by chance.

To love and know that You love too.

To know You would be with me forever.

I know myself and know all about You.

In Endless Hug, it shall stay this way forever.

The Awakening

I opened my eyes to the rays of morning sunlight. This awakening was incomparably more beautiful than I had experienced before; the sunshine had filled my room, gently touching my furniture and computer and encouraging me to get out of bed.

I remembered everything. Andem, the journeys, the magic, but I didn't once think about whether it was a dream or not. In my inner self, I was sure I knew the answer. No question bothered me anymore; I felt I would figure the solution out when I made up the question. Simply, everything seemed natural.

I looked out the window, saw the people, and felt sorry for them that they didn't know everything I did. I wanted to rush to the first person I met on the street to try to transfer this knowledge to them, but the next moment, an inner voice warned me.

Yes. I had a lot to learn since knowledge becomes exactly that once we make it part of our lives if we use it if it becomes a natural element. This task of learning this was still ahead of me. I didn't even know how long this would take in terms of my illusion of time. Still, I did see that it would be a part of me since, in some other, yet to me, invisible dimension, it has already happened.

I opened the window, spread my arms wide, closed my eyes, smiled into the Sun like Andem did, and breathed the fresh morning air.

"Good morning, World!" I shouted and felt such an indescribable joy, which I had never experienced before. "I love you World! I love you very much!"

I knew that this love had filled my soul and that I would still meet Andem too. Possibly in another dimension, after I don't find any goal for myself in this world, but maybe here and now.

Whatever the next phase of my life held in store for me, I knew that every following step would result from my conscious decisions, in which no teacher, parent, religion or law could influence me anymore. I knew that I could create my own reality. However, I also knew that the belief systems I have followed until now – which still, even if only in passing, made up a part of my life – would require all my attention and effort to get rid of. As Andem said: I must invest all my energy into learning for everything to become simple. I will never forget her teachings, and whether I will live with the opportunities shown to me is solely up to me.

Love and Knowledge are infinite. It doesn't just appear out of nothing, and neither does it disappear without a trace. It just exists. That guarantees that we can achieve anything if we don't let our obsolete ideas and visions take control of our lives. We lead our souls' paths according to our own decisions.

So, what most people believe to be reality is just an idea, an illusion. The only actual reality is the Whole. Everything is simple and exists at once, together. Every person can become free, and though they all think they are different from one another, they are the same.

Everybody lives in a personal, separate world whose dimensions provide us with countless opportunities and options, which we can choose from freely, as we wish. We make up the Whole, and the Whole makes up all of us, which can be expressed most simply with one letter: *I.*

Epilogue

The contents of the previous pages might just be a tale, and they might be real. Whatever you believe, you are correct. Whatever your opinion might be, there is one thing that is more important than all else and which casts a shadow over all other things: may you be a blacksmith, a computer programmer, a politician or anything else, you are part of an extraordinary universe, and this empire is just as beautiful as you are unique.

Maybe love and infinite knowledge make up a part of everyone, and we shouldn't follow the laws of people drunk on power. Perhaps we really have the choice of free will; maybe everyone can find complete independence from all other people and events.

The majority never have realised, and probably never will, that they can change their lives at the snap of a finger, that they aren't supposed to see the same things as others, feel the same feelings that other people feel, follow the same rules and laws that other people follow, and that they should only care about their own created world since it contains all that they need.

Those who, in fact, have realised that are probably very happy, but we probably don't know much about them. Either they kept it to themselves and secluded themselves away from society, far away from everyone and everything, to be able to live their lives, or they talked about it, told people that they knew their mind more than science and the laws, and as a result ended up in mental asylums since they couldn't fit into society and conform to society's standards or the sheep mentality in other words. Of course, they also accomplished everything they wanted to in their own worlds and disappeared without a trace.

The choices are available to all of us.

Like now, we always take control of our lives into our hands and achieve freedom or give in to the brainwashing and follow the sheep bell further.

I have made my decision.

"Knowledge is infinite."

Printed in Great Britain
by Amazon

25759265R00067